A Parents Magazine
Read Aloud Original.

Pets I Wouldn't Pick

by Susan Alton Schmeltz
pictures by Ellen Appleby

Parents Magazine Press • New York

To P. and T.,
who keep me laughing — S.A.S.

For my father — E.A.

Publication licensed by Gruner + Jahr USA Publishing

Text Copyright © 1982 by Susan Schmeltz
Illustrations Copyright © 1982 by Ellen Appleby
All rights reserved.
Printed in the United States of America.
10 9 8 7 6 5

Library of Congress Cataloging in Publication Data
Schmeltz, Susan Alton.
Pets I wouldn't pick.
Summary: Poetic pros and cons for a variety of
pet possibilities including frogs, pigs, bats, and elephants.
[1. Pets — Fiction.   2. Stories in rhyme.]
I. Appleby, Ellen, ill.   II. Title.
PZ8.3.S364Pe [E] 81-11071
ISBN 0-8193-1073-5 AACR2
ISBN 0-8193-1074-3 (lib. bdg.)

Choosing pets? Here's free advice:
Don't pick frogs and don't pick mice!

I don't think you'd like a frog.
Frogs don't sit like lumps on logs.
Count on frogs to hip and hop.
And they hardly *ever* stop!

On the counter, on the bed,
On the hat on Grandma's head!

Mice don't hop or jump or slink.
They just nap beneath the sink.
Or play games of hide and seek,
Scaring Sister when they peek.

So before you hear Mom shout,
Why not choose to leave mice out?

There are other pets, you know.
But to squirrels and pigs, say, "No!"

Squirrels are cute as they can be
When they jump from tree to tree.
But in the house a squirrel's a pest,
Hiding nuts and building nests.

What if Auntie comes to call
And trips on acorns in the hall?

Do you think you'd like a pig?
Round and pink and not too big?
What about the piggy's pen?
It won't fit in Daddy's den!

And where will you go to scrub
When pig's mud bath fills your tub?

I'm not through, now please take note:
Owls and bats don't get my vote.

True, an owl will talk to you,
But his only word is "WHOO."
And his feathers fill the air
As he flies from lamp to chair.

How much sleeping could you do
Knowing that he's watching you?

Friends of yours won't spend the night
If your bats give them a fright.
They won't like it when bats zoom
Out of closets in your room!

Bats, I'm sure you will agree,
Just don't fit your family.

Heed my word of warning please:
Don't take spiders! Don't take fleas!

Spiders don't know how to play.
They just spin their webs all day
From the ceiling to the floor,
On the mantle, out the door,

Down the chimney, up the stairs,
Trapping Brother in their snares!

As for fleas, I'm sure you know
They can put on quite a show.
But when the circus star's a flea,
He is hard for you to see.

So your neighbor's dog, Lamar,
Might just walk off with your star.

Two more pets that won't be missed:
Goats and moles, cross off your list!

Goats are good at eating cans.
But did you say you had plans
To get bumped on your back end
Every single time you bend?

You could wind up with your nose
Planted in a yellow rose!

Worst of all about the moles
Is their love of digging holes
In the garden, and the yard,
Making running rather hard.

They leave humps and lumpy hills,
Bringing Daddy gardening bills.

Honestly, here's how I feel:
Skip the beaver! Skip the seal!

Beavers are a busy bunch,
Working while you eat your lunch,
Chomping tables, chewing chairs,
Nibbling railings on the stairs.

Now what will the plumber think
Of those dams in all the sinks?

Your pet seal would make Mom wish
She could lock up every dish.
He will bounce them on his nose
Like the seals in juggling shows.

Get the dust pan! Get the broom!
Two more saucers just went BOOM!

Please be careful, please beware:
Not one elephant! Not one bear!

Elephants would be too hard
For you to squeeze into your yard.
If your bird bath was smashed flat,
You'd know where your pet just sat.

And his tummy's tough to fill.
Could you pay
the grocer's bill?

Honey is a bear's delight.
He can eat it noon or night.
In the winter, in your bed,
With Gramp's nightcap on his head,

Your big, sticky bear will snore,
Then in spring he'll eat some more!

Other pets you should resist
Follow on a handy list:

Alligators, crocodiles —
You can't trust their sneaky smiles.

Porcupines and buffalo —
Where you'd keep them, I don't know!

Walruses and chimpanzees.
Wasps, a hive of honey bees.

Hippos, mother kangaroos.
Aardvarks, eels, and baby gnus.

Whales, giraffes, koala bears.
Hedgehogs that roll down the stairs...

Whew! I'm tired, so could *you* list
Pesky pets that I have missed?

Because it's time for me to feed...

My new pet octopus, McSneed!

About the Author and Artist

SUSAN ALTON SCHMELTZ picked a very unusual pet when she was little: a baby squirrel that her cat had found and brought home. Her mother decided the family could keep him till he grew big enough to go free. The squirrel was smaller than a tea cup and liked curling up in her father's pocket for a nap. "When he ate apple slices, he looked just like my younger brother eating watermelon slices," says Ms. Schmeltz fondly.

Ms. Schmeltz has been writing since 1976 and has had several stories published.

ELLEN APPLEBY thinks hers is the most exceptional of all pets: an Airedale named Nancy. Nancy understands more than 70 words, loves flute music, and enjoys singing along! She is very loyal, but also very independent. "Her single drawback," says Ms. Appleby, "is that she doesn't know how to read."

Ms. Appleby has been illustrating children's books and textbooks since she graduated from the Rhode Island School of Design.